SCIENCE TOOLS

MARLA CONN

Rourke Educational Media

A Division of Carson Dellosa Education

Photo Glossary

balance

beaker

computer

magnet

magnifying glass

 **ruler**

High Frequency Words:

- a
- in
- is
- science
- this
- tools
- use
- we

We use tools in science.

This is a **balance**.

We use tools in science.

This is a **magnifying glass.**

We use tools in science.

This is a **ruler.**

We use tools in science.

This is a computer.

We use tools in science.

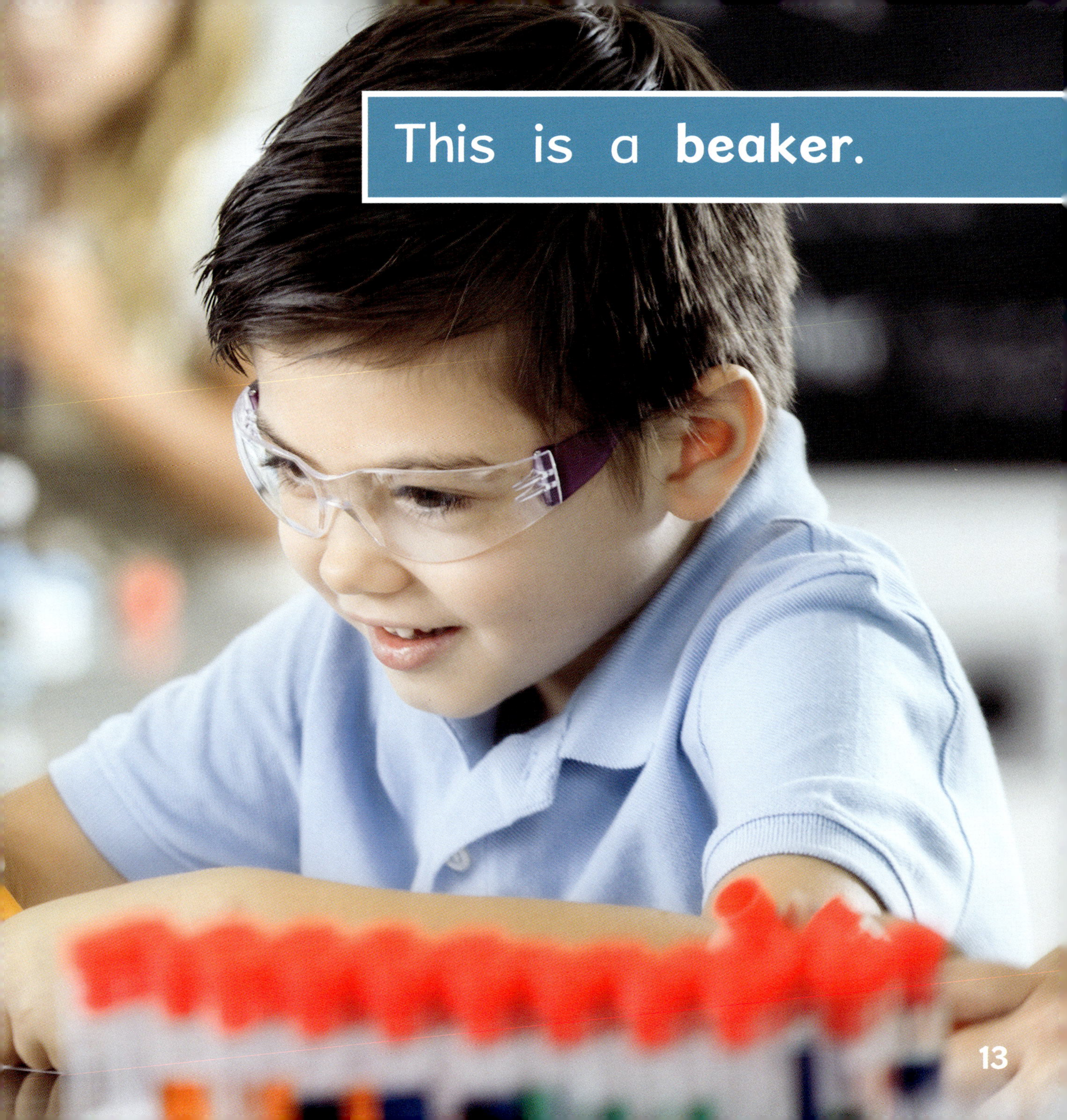

This is a **beaker**.

We use tools in science.

This is a **magnet**.

Activity

1. Go back and read the story with a partner.
2. Discuss the science tools and how they are used.
3. Choose a science tool from the story that matches each sentence.
    - This tool helps me find information.
    - This tool helps me know how long something is.
    - This tool helps me see small objects.
    - This tool helps me know how much liquid there is.
    - This tool helps me know how heavy something is.
    - This tool helps me know if something is metal.